The Adventures of
TAXI DOG

The Adventures of TAXI DOG

by Debra and Sal Barracca
pictures by Mark Buehner

▪▪▪▪▪▪▪▪▪▪▪▪▪▪▪▪▪▪▪▪▪▪

A TRUMPET CLUB SPECIAL EDITION

Published by The Trumpet Club
666 Fifth Avenue, New York, New York 10103

Text copyright © 1990 by Debra and Sal Barracca
Pictures copyright © 1990 by Mark Buehner

ISBN: 0-440-84337-5

This edition published by arrangement with Dial Books for Young Readers,
a division of Penguin Books USA Inc.
Designed by Halcyon Books Inc.
Printed in the United States of America
September 1991

10 9 8 7 6 5 4 3 2 1

UPC

*The art for this book was prepared using oil paints over acrylics.
It was then camera-separated and reproduced in red, yellow, blue, and black.*

For all the homeless and abused creatures of the world—
may they all find peace some day.
D.B. and S.B.

To Mom and Dad
M.B.

My name is Maxi,
I ride in a taxi
Around New York City all day.
I sit next to Jim,
(I belong to him),
But it wasn't always this way.

I grew up in the city,
    All dirty and gritty,
        Looking for food after dark.
I roamed all around,
    Avoiding the pound,
        And lived on my own in the park.

One day a car stopped—
Its tire had popped.
Out stepped a tall man, I could see.
He came over and said
As he patted my head,
"Are you lost? You can come home with me!"

Did I hear right? Oh, boy!
 My tail wagged with joy—
  I jumped right up on the seat!
He said, "My name's Jim,"
 I could ride home with him
  And he'd give me some good food to eat.

I ate and I ate,
    I cleaned the whole plate.
        Then Jim took a scarf of bright red.
He tied it around me,
    So glad that he found me,
        And kissed me on top of my head.

My wish had come true—
I would start life anew.
At last I had a warm home
With someone to love me
And take good care of me—
No longer would I have to roam.

Jim said, "Your name's Maxi,
You'll ride in my taxi,
We'll ride all over the town.
We'll see all the sights,
All the streets and the lights,
We'll go riding uptown and down."

There's so much to see!
　　Every building and tree
　　　　With people and cars everywhere.
All the interesting places—
　　New friends and new faces
　　　　Each time we pick up a fare.

One time a big lady
    Who said she was Sadie
        Was singing that night in a show.
She broke into a song
    And I sang right along—
        You couldn't tell me from the pro!

"To the hospital, quick!
   My wife is quite sick,"
      Cried a man as we stopped for the light,
"Our baby is due!"
      And like lightning we flew—
      We made it in time—what a night!

Sometimes when it's slow
To the airport we go.
We get in the line at the stand
To wait for a fare,
And a hotdog we share
While we watch the planes take off and land.

The door opened wide—
   Guess who jumped inside?
      Two clowns and a chimp they called Murray!
"We're performing at eight
   And our flight came in late—
      To the circus, and please try to hurry!"

We get such big tips
    On most of our trips—
        Jim is surprised at this treat.
But he doesn't know
    That I put on a show
        For the passengers in the backseat!

At the end of each day
    When we've earned our pay,
        We drive the cab back to its spot,
Where our boss named Lou
    Says, "Hi! How'd ya do?
        Have a biscuit!" (He likes me a lot.)

It's just like a dream,
Me and Jim—we're a team!
I'm always there at his side.
We never stand still,
Every day's a new thrill—
Come join us next time for a ride!

ABOUT THE AUTHORS

Debra and Sal Barracca work with many artists and writers of children's books
through their young company, Halcyon Books.
Both are native New Yorkers and they were inspired to write
The Adventures of Taxi Dog after riding in a taxi whose owner kept his dog
with him in the front seat. They will donate a portion of the book's
proceeds to The Fund for Animals in New York City.
The Barraccas live in Croton-on-Hudson, New York with their three cats.

ABOUT THE ARTIST

Mark Buehner grew up in Utah and graduated from Utah State University.
Mr. Buehner works as a freelance illustrator and
The Adventures of Taxi Dog is his first book. He now lives with
his wife and two children in Brooklyn, New York.